Sassy Sisters vs

The Sock Monster

By Jacquese Groves

Illustrated by Karine Makartichan

2020

ChocolateBlue Publishing
Nashville, TN 37203

Publisher: Jacquese Groves, ChocolateBlue, LLC
Illustrator: Karine Makartichan, Pixel's Dream

Printed in the United States of America
First Edition: October 2020

ISBN Paperback: 978-1-7358993-0-5

Library of Congress Control Number: 2020947322

For my sweet daughters, Kennedy and Sydney.
You girls are my greatest inspiration.
I love you both more than you will ever know.

One night, when Mommy and Daddy were folding the laundry, I heard her tell him that the sock monster got our socks again.

"The sock monster?" I whispered.
I ran upstairs to my big sister's room.

"I'm going to see a monster about some socks. Wanna come?"

She laughed and said, "What are you talking about, Sydney?"

She didn't seem too sure about my plan
but since she's my best friend she said,
"Let's go, sistergirl!"

We tiptoed downstairs, past Mommy and Daddy and into the laundry room.

"So what's the plan if we find the sock monster?" Kennedy whispered.

"We're gonna get our socks back, obviously!"

"Aren't you scared?"

"It takes a lot more than a monster to scare me."

Kennedy laughed and said, "Okey-dokey,
I think we need a flashlight."

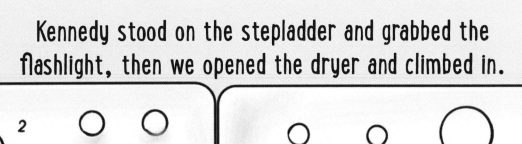

Kennedy stood on the stepladder and grabbed the flashlight, then we opened the dryer and climbed in.

"Turn on the flashlight," I said.

Kennedy turned on the light and we both gasped!
There really was a sock monster and
it was a girl! I thought monsters were boys!"

"I'm Sydney and this is my big sister Kennedy.
This is our dryer, and you're stealing our socks!"

The monster looked surprised and hurt. "No I'm not!"

"Then what's that on your head?" Sydney said.

She pointed to an opening in the bottom of the dryer. I'd never noticed that before.

"What is it?" Kennedy asked.

"Don't tell your mommy and daddy you saw me in here."

"Good, now give them back," Sydney said.

"No can do! I'll put them back when your mommy puts more clothes in the dryer. I want to make sure you don't tell."

"Come on, Sydney, let's just turn around," Kennedy said.
"It's hot in here and I'm ready to get out."

"Okay sis," Sydney said.

We turned around.
We heard the monster making some noise
and then she said, "Okay, you can look now."

She was holding the missing mates
to six pairs of our socks!
I grabbed them and slipped them in my pocket.

She looked at Kennedy's socks
and her face lit up. "Deal!"

We shook hands with the sock monster and
Kennedy and I climbed out of the dryer.

Just as we closed the dryer door,
Mommy came into the laundry room.

Mommy shook her head and laughed.
"Okay girls. Did you find him?"

The girls looked at each other,
and Sydney spoke first.
"Maybe we did, maybe we didn't."

"But don't worry," Kennedy said.
"I don't think any more of
our socks will go missing."

CPSIA information can be obtained at www.ICGtesting.com
Printed in the USA
LVIW010248171120
671898LV00008B/159